Annie Bananie

by Leah Komaiko · illustrated by Laura Cornell

HarperTrophy
A Division of HarperCollinsPublishers

For Annie
L.K.

For my parents
L.C.

ANNIE BANANIE
Text copyright © 1987 by Leah Komaiko
Illustrations copyright © 1987 by Laura Cornell
Printed in Mexico. All rights reserved.

Library of Congress Cataloging-in-Publication Data
Komaiko, Leah.
    Annie Bananie.
    Summary: Sad because her best friend, Annie
Bananie, is moving away, a little girl remembers all
the fun they had together.
    (1. Friendship—Fiction.   2. Moving, Household—
Fiction.   3. Stories in rhyme)   I. Cornell, Laura, ill.
II. Title.
PZ8.3.K835An 1987   (E)   86-45767
ISBN 0-06-023259-5
ISBN 0-06-023261-7 (lib. bdg.)
ISBN 0-06-443198-3 (pbk.)

Designed by Constance Fogler
First Harper Trophy edition, 1989.

Annie Bananie,
My best friend,

Said we'd be friends to the end.

Made me brush my teeth with mud,
Sign my name in cockroach blood,

Tie my brother to the trees,
Made me tickle bumblebees.

Promised we would always play.

Now Annie Bananie's going away.

Annie Bananie
Wouldn't be
Annie Bananie if it weren't for me!

She was Ann
From outer space.

I scrubbed the freckles off her face.

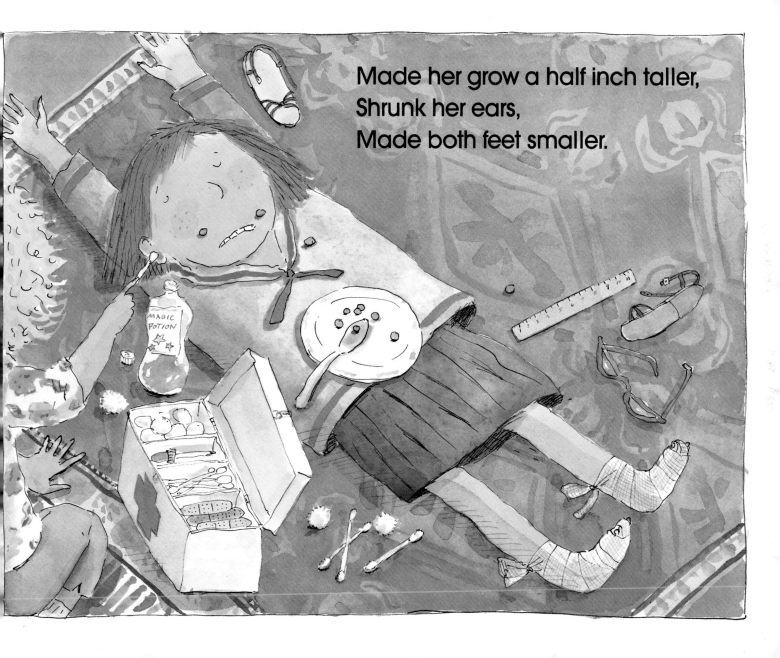

Made her grow a half inch taller,
Shrunk her ears,
Made both feet smaller.

Brought her out for all to see—

Princess Annie Ba-nanie.

Annie Bananie,
Do you think it's good
Leaving your whole neighborhood?

Who will feed your porcupine?
Who will swing from your clothesline?

Annie Bananie,
Do not cry—

Even best friends say good-by.

Make some new friends,
Try to write,

And when you are in bed at night,
Remember...

You will never ever ever

Find a friend who's half as clever.

You will never ever find
Someone who's as sweet and kind.

No you'll never

Ever ever

Never ever

Ever

Find another friend like me.